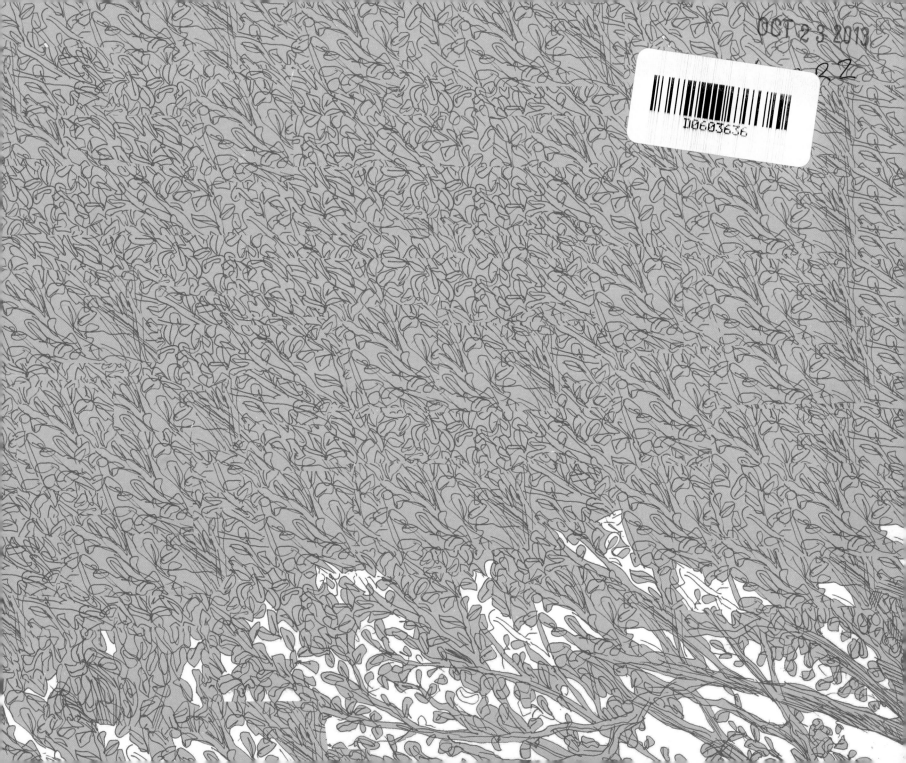

In the Tree House

For Johnny, Jimmy and Patty and all that we shared.
For Esther for everything else. — A.L.

To my big brother, Aleksandar. — D.P.

Kids Can Press acknowledges the financial support of the Government of Ontario, through the Ontario Media Development Corporation's Ontario Book Initiative; the Ontario Arts Council; the Canada Council for the Arts; and the Government of Canada, through the CBF, for our publishing activity.

Published in Canada by
Kids Can Press Ltd.
25 Dockside Drive
Toronto, ON M5A 0B5

Published in the U.S. by
Kids Can Press Ltd.
2250 Military Road
Tonawanda, NY 14150

www.kidscanpress.com

The artwork in this book was rendered in pen and ink and colored in Photoshop.
The text is set in Electra LT Std.

Edited by Yvette Ghione
Designed by Marie Bartholomew

This book is smyth sewn casebound.
Manufactured in Shenzhen, China, in 11/2012 through Asia Pacific Offset.

CM 13 0 9 8 7 6 5 4 3 2 1

Library and Archives Canada Cataloguing in Publication

Larsen, Andrew, 1960–
In the tree house / written by Andrew Larsen ; illustrated by Dušan Petričić.

ISBN 978-1-55453-635-1 (bound)

I. Petričić, Dušan II. Title.

PS8623.A77I68 2013   jC813'.6   C2012-905180-2

Kids Can Press is a CORUS™ Entertainment company

In the Tree House

Andrew Larsen   Dušan Petričić

Kids Can Press

It's hot. Really hot.

I crunch on an ice cube to cool off.

There's more ice melting in the bowl beside me.

I can see the whole neighborhood from up here.

It's pretty nice.

There are lots of big, old trees.

But there's only one tree house.

I was so excited when we moved here last year.

We finally had our own house with our own backyard.

And I finally had my own room.

I had trouble falling asleep at first.

I guess I missed sharing a room with my brother.

I tried counting sheep but that didn't work.

I just lay awake, picturing more
sheep than I could count.

So I started planning
tree houses.

I planned tree houses that could turn into flying ships at the flick of a switch.

I planned tree houses with secret slides for quick getaways.

I planned one tree house that had two levels, one for me and one for my brother.

I told my brother about my tree houses,
and pretty soon he was drawing his own.
"Can I see them?" I asked one day.

His drawings were really good.

He said mine were good, too.

We showed them to our dad.

"When I was a kid," he said, "I wanted a tree house more than anything else in the world."

"Did you build one?" my brother asked.

"Nope," Dad answered. "I never had my own backyard."

"So what did you do?" I asked.

"I made plans," he said. "Just like you."

We started building our tree house the next morning.

It was dark when we finally finished.

"Why aren't there any stars?" I asked between gulps of lemonade.

"They're up there," Dad said. "We just can't see them."

He explained how the lights from the city make the sky too bright for us to see the stars shine.

So we watched the twinkling lights of our sleepy neighborhood instead.

My brother and I spent most of
that summer in the tree house.

It was the best summer ever.

We had comics.

We had cards.

Dad even got us a couple of flashlights.

This summer has been different, though.

Very different.

My brother doesn't spend any time in the tree house.

He hardly spends any time with me.

He's too busy with his friends.

He says I'm too little to hang out with them.

He doesn't even let me in his room anymore.

So now I'm the king of the castle.
I can do whatever I want up here.

Lights go on all over the neighborhood.

Televisions glow in the windows.

Air conditioners hum.

It sounds like I'm inside a fridge.

It *feels* like I'm inside an oven.

I blink, and then —

Everything is dark.

Everything is quiet.

"Are you all right up there?"

Dad calls from the house.

"The power's gone out."

"I'm okay," I answer.

The melting ice crackles in the bowl.

Something sparkles overhead.

The night sky is filled with stars,
more than I can count.

The neighbors are coming out of their houses.

Some have candles. Some have flashlights.

They're all talking and laughing in the dark. It's a party!

"Who wants to play hide-and-seek?"

a kid from down the street calls out.

"Who wants ice cream?" a grown-up asks.
"Come and get it before it melts!"

I'm thinking about climbing down when I hear
someone coming up the ladder.

It's my brother.

"Hey," he says. "Can I hang out?"

"Okay," I answer. "Come on up."

"What are you doing up here?" he asks.

"Are you hiding?"

"Just thinking," I answer.

"This place is looking good," he says.

"Thanks," I say proudly. "Want some lemonade?"

He sips his drink without saying anything.
I wonder what he's thinking.

"Are those new Sidekick Jimmy comics?" he asks,
finally. "I used to love those."

"Check out this one," I say. "Jimmy rescues his
dad from a pit of quicksand."

"Cool," he says, reaching for a flashlight and
settling in for a read.

"Cool," I say, crunching another ice cube.

The blackout ends a couple of hours later.

The party is over.

The neighbors blow out their candles and go back inside like nothing has happened, like it's just another night.

Not us.

We read comics.

We play crazy eights.

We play war.

And then we build a house of cards.

We stay up and watch the twinkling lights of our sleepy neighborhood.